Magic Pony Carousel
Book 4

JEWEL
THE MIDNIGHT PONY

Magic Pony Carousel
Book 4

JEWEL
THE MIDNIGHT PONY

Poppy Shire

Illustrations by Ron Berg

HarperTrophy®

An Imprint of HarperCollins*Publishers*

With special thanks to Holly Skeet

★ ★ ★ ★ ★

JEWEL THE MIDNIGHT PONY

www.harpercollinschildrens.com

Library of Congress Cataloging-in-Publication Data
Shire, Poppy.
    Jewel the midnight pony / [by Poppy Shire ; illustrations by
Ron Berg]. — 1st Harper Trophy ed.
        p. cm. — (The magic pony carousel ; bk. 4)
    Summary: When Sophie rides the magic pony carousel, she
and her carousel pony are whisked back in time to stop a robber
and save a new friend.
    ISBN 978-0-06-083788-4 (pbk.)
    [1. Robbers and outlaws—Fiction. 2. Ponies—Fiction.
3. Magic—Fiction. 4. Space and time—Fiction. 5. Friendship—
Fiction.] I. Berg, Ron, ill. II. Title.
PZ7.S55795Je 2008   2007020827
[Fic]—dc22   CIP
                                                          AC

Typography by Sasha Illingworth
❖
First Harper Trophy edition, 2008

★ ★ ★ ★ ★

Magic Pony Carousel
Book 4

JEWEL
THE MIDNIGHT PONY

Chapter One

"Got it!" Sophie waved her long bamboo pole. It had a yellow plastic duck swinging madly on the hook at the end.

"Well done!" said her mom.

Sophie's dad unhooked the duck and handed it to the woman standing on the other side of the inflatable pool. Lots of bright yellow ducks bobbed on the water, waiting to be hooked. The woman smiled at Sophie and told her to choose a prize.

Sophie picked a key ring in the shape of a pretty jet-black pony with a tiny white dot on its forehead. She loved ponies more than anything else in the world! "Thank you!" she said to the woman in charge.

Beside her, there was a crash as Sophie's little sister Molly threw down her bamboo pole. "This is a stupid game!" Molly grumbled. "I can't hook any of the ducks. They keep swimming away!"

Sophie sighed. Molly was only four, and she got very annoyed when she couldn't do everything Sophie did.

"Let's go and find something else," said their dad. He took Sophie and Molly by the hands and they wandered farther into the fair. It was very busy, and Sophie held tightly to her dad's hand. She put her other hand in her pocket to check if her pony key ring was still there. The little jet-black pony felt warm and smooth underneath her fingers.

There were rides and games *everywhere*!

Sophie thought she'd never be able to decide what to go on next. Her mom pointed to a stall where you had to kick a soccer ball into a goal to win prizes. But Sophie didn't think she could win a better prize than her pony key ring, so she shook her head.

Just then, she spotted a pointy golden roof peeping out from behind the soccer ball game. Tugging her dad's hand, she led him over.

"Look!" Sophie cried. "It's a pony carousel!" It was the prettiest fairground ride she had ever seen. The wooden ponies were really lifelike, their eyes twinkling and their tails floating out behind them.

"Would you like to have a turn?" asked Sophie's mom.

"Yes, please!" Sophie said. There was nothing she wanted more than to ride on the carousel, holding one of the twisty golden poles.

But Molly had spotted something else. "I want to go on the giant teacups!" she said, pointing.

Sophie stared at her sister in surprise. How could giant spinning teacups be better than the beautiful pony carousel? Molly started to drag their dad toward the teacups. Now Sophie wouldn't be able to go on the carousel!

Her mom bent down and gave her shoulders a squeeze. "Shall we stay here while your dad takes Molly on the teacups?" she said. Sophie nodded eagerly.

She walked to the bottom of the steps leading up to the carousel. There were so many ponies! There was a stocky white pony, with a stiff mane and bells and ribbons on his harness—the kind of pony Sophie had seen pulling sleighs in pictures. Then she spotted a handsome bay pony with brave brown eyes and a tail that flowed all the way down to the floor. He had an old-fashioned saddle as though he was a medieval knight's pony.

Then Sophie gasped out loud. One of the ponies looked exactly like her key ring! He was jet-black—the color of a dark, velvety night—and he had a perfect diamond of white on his forehead. When Sophie peered closer, she saw a little name scroll hanging from the golden pole on his back. It read JEWEL! It was the perfect name for such a beautiful pony.

Someone coughed politely close by, making Sophie jump. A tall gentleman was standing behind her. He was grandly dressed in a red velvet suit and a red-and-green-striped top hat. He bowed to Sophie, sweeping the hat from his head.

"Welcome to Barker's Magic Pony Carousel!" he declared. His blue eyes twinkled. "My name is Mr. Barker."

Sophie stared at him. "Did you just say *Magic*

Pony Carousel?" she said.

Mr. Barker grinned. "Oh yes! Most definitely magic. Would you like a ride on the carousel?"

"I'd love one!" Sophie gasped.

"Well, I have just a few tickets left for the next ride," he said. He reached into his pocket and took out some tiny pieces of pink paper. "The name of your pony is written on the ticket you choose, Sophie. Think hard about which pony you'd like it to be!" Mr. Barker held out the tickets to Sophie, along with a magnifying glass. "Pick one! And have a look at it with the magnifying glass. The writing can be a little hard to read sometimes," he explained.

Sophie thought hard about the midnight-black pony that looked like her key ring. Then, with trembling fingers she chose one of the little pink tickets. She lifted the magnifying glass and peered at the tiny piece of paper. The swirly writing *was* hard to read—but it definitely said Jewel.

"It's Jewel!" she told him excitedly.

"Ah! That's a very special pony." Mr. Barker beamed. "Now, quickly, on you get. We're ready to start. Climb aboard, everyone! All aboard the Magic Pony Carousel!"

Sophie ran up the steps and wove her way through the other wooden ponies until she reached Jewel. "I'm so glad your name was on my ticket!" she whispered, stroking the white diamond on his forehead. The painted wood felt silky under her fingers. Jewel's dark eyes seemed to look straight into hers, as though he was glad, too. Sophie gave him a quick kiss on the nose, then climbed into the saddle.

Mr. Barker checked that everyone was on his or her pony before he twirled a big golden handle to start the carousel. There was a grating noise,

then music rang out, and Sophie felt Jewel soar into the air as the carousel moved off. She gripped the golden pole tightly and waved to her mom as she whirled past her. The fairground slipped by in a blur of silvery-lilac light, the tinkling music filled Sophie's ears, and the crowds seemed to fade away.

Sophie blinked. The other girls on their wooden ponies had vanished, too, and she and Jewel were galloping through swirls of sparkling mist. The sunlight dimmed until they were surrounded by velvety black shadows. . . .

Suddenly, Sophie knew they weren't in the fairground anymore!

Chapter Two

The sparkly mist cleared away, leaving Sophie and Jewel standing alone at a crossroads on a grassy heath. There was just one house in the distance, with a dim light burning in the window. From somewhere far away, Sophie could hear a church clock striking—ten, eleven, twelve strokes. It was midnight! Sophie looked around, feeling utterly bewildered. A minute ago she'd been at a noisy, colorful fairground—and now she was in the middle of nowhere, in the middle of the night! She patted Jewel's wooden neck for comfort.

To her amazement, he snorted and shook his head. Jewel wasn't wooden at all! He was a real pony. Sophie stroked his thick, warm mane, and he reached his head around to nuzzle at her hand.

"What's going on?" Sophie breathed. "Where *are* we?"

As her eyes got used to the darkness, she realized she was no longer wearing her favorite jeans with the sequined butterflies and her pink T-shirt. Instead, she was dressed in shiny black satin breeches, soft leather riding boots, and a white shirt with ruffles on the collar and cuffs. Hanging from her shoulders was a magnificent black velvet cloak lined with purple silk. Sophie wriggled her feet in the close-fitting boots. She felt dressed for adventure!

A flash of white among the trees by the road caught her eye, and she walked Jewel over to see what it was. Jewel didn't seem very happy about walking anywhere. Sophie could feel him trembling beneath her, and his bit jangled as he nervously tossed his head. "Hey, boy," Sophie murmured, patting his neck again. "It's okay, we're just going to look at that piece of paper." Sophie had ridden nervous ponies before, and she knew she had to take everything very slowly and not force Jewel on when he was frightened.

The flash of white turned out to be a poster nailed to the tree. Sophie edged Jewel really close so she could read it. Maybe it would help her work out where she was!

REWARD

HAVE YOU SEEN THIS MAN?

Sophie gasped. It was a wanted poster! Sophie eased it off its nail so she could read it better in the moonlight. Below the heavy black letters was

a drawing of a scary-looking man, with thick black eyebrows and an ugly scar down the side of his face. Next to his picture were some drawings of jewelry, including a beautiful golden locket with a pattern of roses. More writing explained that the locket had been stolen from the Earl of Sussex. It contained tiny paintings of the earl and his wife.

At the very bottom of the poster was a message:

LARGE REWARD IN RETURN FOR INFORMATION
ON THE WHEREABOUTS OF
THE VILLAINOUS ROBBER GALLOPING JIM.
REWARD ALSO OFFERED FOR THE RETURN
OF A PRICELESS LOCKET
STOLEN FROM THE EARL OF SUSSEX.

Sophie shuddered. "I wouldn't like to meet Galloping Jim tonight," she said out loud, hooking the poster back on its nail.

"Me neither," someone replied.

Sophie nearly jumped out of the saddle in shock. Who said that? She looked around, thinking someone must have crept up behind them, but she was still on her own.

On her own, that is, except for Jewel.

Sophie frowned. Then she leaned forward and whispered in Jewel's ear, "Was that you?"

Jewel nodded.

Sophie sat back up quickly. "But ponies can't talk! What's happening?"

Jewel tossed his mane. "Didn't Mr. Barker tell you it was a Magic Pony Carousel?" he said. "All ponies can talk, but most people don't know how to listen. The carousel's magic ticket means you can understand me. Anyone else would just think I was whinnying."

Sophie felt a bubble of excitement growing

inside her. "I knew there was something special about that pony carousel!" she said.

"The carousel has brought us here to help someone," Jewel explained. "But don't worry— the magic will take us back before your mom notices you've gone."

"Who are we meant to help?" Sophie looked around. "There's no one else here!"

Jewel snorted. "I'm not sure, exactly. But we'll know when we find the right person. I just wish it wasn't so dark," he muttered. "Why do we have to have an adventure in the middle of the night?"

"Don't be scared, Jewel," said Sophie. She reached forward and rubbed the soft bit of hair behind his ears.

Jewel stretched out his neck. "Ooh, that feels nice. A little higher . . . Wait! What's that?"

A rattling, thudding noise was coming from farther along the road. Sophie held the reins tightly to stop Jewel from running away.

The noise grew louder and louder until an old-fashioned coach burst out of the shadows, pulled by four magnificent gray horses. Their harnesses jingled and their tails streamed out behind them as they galloped along.

"We'd better get out of the way," Jewel said nervously, and he stepped into the shadow of the trees.

The coach was going so fast that the lanterns hanging on each corner swung wildly from side to side. Peering forward, Sophie could see the passengers inside hanging on for dear life. The coach didn't look a comfy ride on such a stony, rutted track.

As the coach drew level with Sophie and Jewel, a chestnut pony shot out from behind some trees on the other side of the road. A girl the same age as Sophie was urging the pony on as fast as she could.

Sophie stared at her in surprise. "She came

out of nowhere!" she said to Jewel. "Do you think she wants to get on the coach?"

"I don't think so!" Jewel hissed back. "Watch!"

"Stand and deliver!" the girl called faintly, and her pony reared and neighed.

But the driver was going too fast to notice the girl and the pony lurking in the shadows. The coach just sped on, its wooden wheels bouncing over the stones.

As the coach and its passengers rattled safely away, Sophie got a chance to look at the girl properly. She looked almost ghostly in the moonlight, with her pale face and mass of brown curls. She had a dark, three-pointed hat pulled low over her face, and she was wearing a flowing cloak, similar to Sophie's—and as she turned her pony, Sophie spotted a black satin mask across her eyes.

She was a robber!

Chapter Three

Sophie had read about robbers in her favorite book of horse stories, but she'd never heard of a girl being one!

Suddenly an owl hooted, and Jewel leaped sideways in surprise. Sophie tried to keep him still, but it was too late. His hooves clattered on the stony ground, and the robber looked around sharply.

"Who's there?" she called.

Sophie gasped. "Jewel, what should we do?" she whispered.

"I don't think we can run away," he whispered

back. "She knows we're here now." With a snort, he stepped out of the shadows. Sophie felt very proud of him for being so brave.

The robber rode over to them. "Who are you?" she demanded.

"We're . . . er . . . travelers," Sophie stammered.

Suddenly, to Sophie's astonishment, the girl laughed. "I missed it again, didn't I?" she said.

Sophie nodded, still too startled to speak.

The girl grinned. "Never mind! I was watching an owl in the wood, and I lost track of time. Not that I wanted to stop the coach anyway. They'll all get home safe, with their money and jewels."

Sophie felt very confused. "You didn't want to stop the coach?"

The girl sighed. "I was supposed to stop it and steal the passengers' money. But I'm no good at

it. I must be the worst robber ever." She smiled at Sophie. "I'm Lucy, by the way. What's your name?"

"I'm Sophie, and this is Jewel."

"Hello, Jewel." Lucy leaned forward to stroke Jewel's white diamond. Suddenly she stopped and looked anxious. "You won't report me, will you, Sophie? If you went to the parish constable, I would get into terrible trouble."

Sophie guessed that the parish constable was a bit like the police. Her granddad was a policeman. He had told her that the police had started almost two hundred years ago, when people decided to take care of law and order in their individual villages. She and Jewel must have traveled back in time over two hundred years!

Lucy was still looking very worried. Sophie shook her head. "Don't worry, I won't say anything. Besides, I don't think you can get into much trouble for *not* stopping a coach!"

Lucy grinned again, her teeth flashing white in the shadows. "I suppose not. I'd better get home now. Where are you staying?"

"I don't know," Sophie admitted. It was chilly, and the dark heath was a bit spooky for camping out. Jewel stamped his hoof, as though he didn't fancy a night outside either.

Lucy looked at her hopefully. "Well, why don't you come and stay at my uncle's house?"

Sophie hesitated. She ran her fingers through Jewel's mane, trying to think. Could she trust Lucy? She seemed nice, but she dressed like a robber, even if she didn't really want to rob coaches. . . .

"Please come!" said Lucy. "My uncle will be out playing cards, and there isn't anyone else to keep me company. It would be so nice to have someone to talk to."

Sophie was very tempted, but she needed to ask Jewel first. "Hold on a minute—I, er, I need to check Jewel's girths," she said. "His saddle feels a bit loose." She wheeled Jewel around. They walked a little way and Sophie dismounted so she could talk to Jewel while she pretended to tighten his girths.

"What do you think, Jewel? Lucy seems really nice, and we don't have anywhere else to stay."

Jewel nodded. "You're right. I hope there's a nice warm stable for me! And maybe when we get to Lucy's house, we'll find whoever it is we need to help."

Sophie led him back to where Lucy was waiting. "We'd love to stay with you, thank you," she said.

Lucy jumped off her pony and gave Sophie a hug. "Oh, I'm so glad! You can share my room, and Jewel can go in the stable with Brown Bess."

She stroked her pony's mane, and Bess snorted happily. She was a big chestnut pony with a pretty, intelligent face. She seemed friendly, too, as she stretched her nose forward to nuzzle Jewel.

They climbed back onto their ponies, and Lucy led the way, deeper into the trees. Jewel shivered as the shadows swallowed them up.

Sophie patted his neck. "Not long now, Jewel."

After a while, Lucy slowed down and twisted around in the saddle to look at Sophie. "We're nearly there, but the path's really narrow and there are lots of brambles, so watch out."

Sophie could hardly see the path at all! She had to concentrate very hard to steer Jewel between the prickly bushes. Sophie was peering so carefully at the path that it was a shock when Lucy said, "Here we are."

Sophie saw Lucy dismount and point toward a gap in the brambles. She looked and caught her breath. They were standing in front of the most rickety, tumbledown house she had ever seen!

Chapter Four

The house looked as if no one had lived there for a very long time. Brambles sprawled over the fence into the garden. The red-tiled roof was full of holes, and several of the windows were broken. The green paint on the front door was peeling away in long curls. Sophie began to think that she wasn't going to get a very comfy night's sleep.

"The stable's this way," said Lucy, leading them around the side of the house. The stables badly needed a coat of paint, but at least the stalls were dry, and fresh straw lay thickly on the floor.

"Will you be all right here?" Sophie whispered

as she took off Jewel's saddle and bridle.

Jewel looked around. He swished his tail happily when he spotted a rack full of sweet-smelling hay. "Yum!" he said. "Don't worry about me. I'll be fine." He walked over and started munching a mouthful of hay.

Sophie felt very relieved. She covered Jewel with a snug-looking rug, made sure he had plenty of water, and then gave him one last hug before leaving the stable.

She followed Lucy to the front door and waited while she took a heavy iron key from underneath a large round stone by the doorstep. Staring up at the cracked windows, Sophie couldn't help wondering if she would have been more comfortable staying in Jewel's stable.

As Lucy pushed open the door, Sophie let out a gasp.

"Looks different in here, doesn't it?" said Lucy.

Inside, the tumbledown house was more like

a palace! Sophie stepped through the doorway and stared around. Her feet sank into a rich red carpet, and the walls were covered in gorgeous red-and-gold-striped silk. A chandelier hung from the ceiling, the small glass drops twinkling in the candlelight.

"This is amazing!" Sophie said. She wished Jewel could see this, too.

She walked into a room leading off the hallway and went over to stroke the soft velvet curtains that hung all the way down to the floor. She noticed a carved wooden box on a pretty table with spindly legs. The box was overflowing with beautiful jewelry, from brooches and rings studded with glowing jewels to a long pearl necklace that spilled over the edge of the table like a silvery snake.

Sophie turned to Lucy, who was watching her from the doorway. "The house is so beautiful!

But why is it falling down on the outside?"

"My uncle keeps the outside of the house looking ruined so people think there's no one living here," Lucy explained. "He doesn't like visitors." Before she could say anything else, a little silver clock standing next to the jewelry box began to chime. "We'd better go to bed," said Lucy. "I have to get up early to make my uncle's breakfast."

She led Sophie up the stairs to a pretty bedroom with pale blue walls the exact color of the summer sky. Two beds stood side by side under the window, draped in matching blue and silver eiderdowns.

"I wish my bedroom was like this," said Sophie. "It would be so cool to have two beds. I'd have friends stay over all the time!"

Lucy was taking a nightgown out of a drawer. She stopped and looked at Sophie, biting her lip.

"Actually, no one has ever slept in that other bed," she confessed. "My uncle doesn't like me having any friends." She handed Sophie the nightgown and smiled. "I'm really glad I met you."

Sophie felt sorry for her new friend. "Isn't there anyone you can play with?" she asked, as she got changed into the pretty embroidered nightgown. It was very different from her pink-and-white spotted pajamas at home.

Lucy jumped into her bed and pulled the sky-blue and silver cover around her knees. "There are some children in the village who I'd like to be friends with, but my uncle Jim would never let me play with them."

Sophie frowned. "Why not?"

Lucy looked down at her knees and fiddled with a loose thread on the eiderdown. Sophie guessed Lucy didn't like talking about her uncle, so she didn't ask any more questions. She snuggled into her cozy bed and put her head on the big fluffy pillow. This was the most exciting adventure she'd ever had!

Sophie woke to find sunlight streaming in through the curtains. Lucy was still curled up in bed, fast asleep. Downstairs, someone was shouting crossly. Sophie slipped out of bed and tiptoed along the landing. Peering over the banister, she caught sight of a tall, broad-shouldered man striding down the hall.

"Where's my breakfast, Lucy?" he yelled.

Sophie ducked back into the bedroom. She had a feeling Lucy's uncle wouldn't be too happy to have an unexpected guest.

Lucy was standing beside her bed, pulling on her clothes. "Sorry! Got to go!" she gasped to Sophie before she vanished out of the door, carrying her boots under her arm.

Sophie got dressed and crept down the stairs to the kitchen. Lucy was frying eggs in a big pan over a fire. Her uncle was nowhere to be seen.

"Can I help?" Sophie asked.

"Could you make some toast?" Lucy pointed to some thick slices of bread on the table. "The toasting fork's over there."

Sophie gulped. She'd never tried to make toast by stabbing the bread with a big metal fork and holding it over a coal fire! The first slice fell into the flames, but Sophie soon got the hang of it. Soon the kitchen was filled with the delicious smell of warm, crispy bread. Sophie and Lucy loaded the breakfast onto a big gold tray and Lucy carefully carried it into the dining room.

Sophie watched from behind the door as Lucy put the tray down in front of her uncle. As he

glanced up to speak to Lucy, Sophie's heart jumped into her mouth. She had seen that face before!

Lucy's uncle was Galloping Jim, the famous robber!

Chapter Five

"Why didn't you tell me your uncle was Galloping Jim?" Sophie burst out, as Lucy came back into the kitchen with the empty tray.

"You recognized him, then?" Lucy said, looking very upset.

Sophie nodded. "I saw a poster last night."

"I didn't want to scare you off," Lucy explained sadly. "I thought you might run away! I just wanted a friend, even if it was only for one night." To Sophie's dismay Lucy started to cry.

"Oh don't, please!" said Sophie, going over to

give her a hug. She found a crisp white handker-chief in the pocket of her breeches and handed it to Lucy. "Is that why you have to be a robber?"

Lucy nodded.

"But why does your uncle want *you* to hold up the coaches?" Sophie asked. "He's a robber himself!"

"He's too well-known." Lucy blew her nose. "He can't risk being seen holding up a coach or Mr. Joy the village constable would catch him."

A shout from the dining room made them stop talking. Lucy darted off, wiping her eyes. Sophie followed her along the hall and peeked around the door.

"So, my girl, what did you get last night? A bag of gold coins? Some jewels? Hand it over!" Galloping Jim bellowed.

Lucy hung her head. "I didn't manage to stop the coach," she confessed.

"What, again?" roared her uncle. Sophie shuddered as Galloping Jim's eyebrows drew together in a fearsome frown. "You're worse than useless!" He banged his fist down on the table, making the plates jump. "It's no good. I'll have to go out myself tonight. I'm not letting you mess this one up, Lucy."

"Whose coach is it?" Lucy asked.

Galloping Jim spoke through a mouthful of toast, spraying crumbs everywhere. "Lady Amelia Grey is off to a ball in her private coach. She'll be wearing all her best jewels! And I'll be waiting at the crossroads when her coach goes by." He sighed. "Really, if I have to hold up the coaches myself, I don't know why I bother letting you stay here. Go on, be off," he snarled. Lucy dodged as he threw a silver salt cellar after her.

Back in the kitchen, Sophie watched Lucy pace angrily up and down. "I can't let him hold up Lady Amelia's coach! But what can I do? If Uncle Jim gets any crosser with me, he'll send me to the orphanage!" She swept her hand along the table, shoving the gold plates and engraved knives and forks to the floor with a crash. Then she sighed, got down on her knees, and started to clean up.

"There must be something we can do," said Sophie, as she bent down to help Lucy pick up the plates.

Lucy tried to smile. "Only washing the dishes," she said.

Sophie decided to talk to Jewel. She grabbed a couple of apples from the bowl on the table and dashed outside, telling Lucy she was going to feed the ponies.

Jewel was dozing in his stall next to Bess. Sophie gently stroked them awake and fed them each an apple while she broke the news.

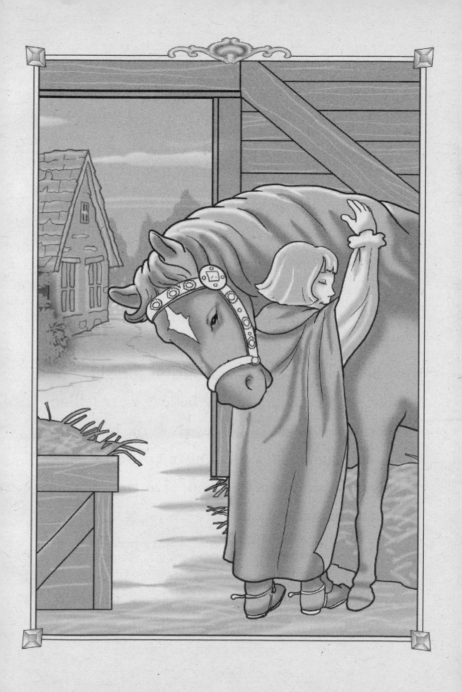

"Galloping Jim is Lucy's uncle?" Jewel gasped.

"Yes, and he's going to hold up a coach tonight! Jewel, you know you said we were sent here to help someone? Well, I think we have to save Lucy from her uncle!"

Jewel nodded. "But how?" He thoughtfully chewed a mouthful of apple. "I know! Didn't Lucy mention a constable in the village?"

"That's right. His name is Mr. Joy."

Jewel scraped his hoof on the floor. "We need to help him catch Galloping Jim tonight. But how can we make Mr. Joy believe we're telling the truth? A house full of jewels in the middle of a forest sounds like something out of a fairy tale!" Suddenly his ears pricked up. "Do you remember that poster you saw on a tree?"

"Of course!" said Sophie. "That's how I recognized Galloping Jim."

"Ah, but what *else* was on it?" Jewel prompted.

Sophie pictured the poster in her head. "Well,

there was a drawing of the locket that was stolen from the Earl of Sussex. . . . Jewel, you're a genius!" She threw her arms around his neck. "If I can find the locket in Galloping Jim's house, I can show it to Mr. Joy. And I bet I know where it is. There's a jewelry box in the living room overflowing with necklaces and things. I'll go and look now."

"I'll wait here," Jewel called after her, "and then we can go and find Mr. Joy."

Sophie ran back to the house. Lucy was still scrubbing pans in the kitchen.

"Don't worry! We've got a plan!" Sophie whispered as she sped past.

She tiptoed into the hallway. She couldn't risk making any noise in case Uncle Jim found her. As she tiptoed past the dining room she peeked around the door. He was drinking a cup of tea, scowling.

Sophie knew she had to be quick. She crept into the living room and went over to the table.

As she sorted through the jewelry, she noticed a beautiful chain like a fine gold rope. Could it be the locket? Suddenly she heard a chair scraping in the dining room. Galloping Jim was getting up! She pulled frantically at the chain—yes, this was it! On the end of the chain was a large gold oval, carved with delicate roses, that opened up to reveal two tiny portraits.

Sophie raced back to the kitchen, her heart thumping. "Lucy, I have to get to the village! Which way is it?"

Lucy looked alarmed. "You need to go back along the path, then turn left by the big oak tree. You're not going to tell the constable about Uncle Jim, are you? Sophie, you mustn't!"

A tiny flicker of doubt went through Sophie's mind. Were she and Jewel doing the right thing? Lucy seemed so frightened. *I have to do this,* she told herself firmly. Lucy couldn't stay here with her wicked uncle forever—she had to be rescued. This was what the carousel had sent her and Jewel here for.

"Lucy, it will be all right. I promise it will. Just trust me and Jewel. Meet us in the village this evening." Sophie shot out of the back door, then popped her head back around. "And try not to worry!"

Chapter Six

Sophie saddled up Jewel and rode back down the brambly path. She was a bit confused about which oak tree Lucy meant, but Jewel helped her out. He sniffed the air. "This way! I can smell smoke from the village chimneys."

They followed a twisty path through the woods. Not far from the edge of the forest there were some little white houses with thatched roofs.

Sophie heard a strange clinking sound. "What's that?" she said.

Jewel snorted. "It's the blacksmith's hammer,"

he explained. "We must be close to the forge."

They followed the noise to a long, low building. The door was open to reveal a fire burning brightly. A little boy with curly black hair was pumping a set of bellows to make the flames leap higher. Outside, a tall, white-haired man with a bright red scarf around his neck was nailing a shoe to the hoof of a stocky brown and white horse. The blacksmith! He looked familiar, but Sophie couldn't work out why. She watched as he fixed the hot shoe in place. It gave off a hiss of steam, but the horse stood very still.

A girl about the same age as Sophie came running around the corner. She stopped when she saw Sophie and smiled. "Hello!" she said. "Are you looking for someone?"

"Yes, please," said Sophie. "I don't suppose you know where I'd find Mr. Joy, do you? The parish constable?"

The girl laughed, her eyes sparkling. "You're in luck! That's his horse being shod, and he's the one holding the bridle." Then she ran off again, flashing another smile at Sophie.

The blacksmith carefully lowered the horse's hoof to the ground and straightened up, giving Sophie a friendly wink. She was sure she knew him! Of course—he looked just like Mr. Barker from the carousel!

The man holding the horse smiled at Sophie. "Did I hear you tell Ellen you wanted to talk to me?"

Sophie nodded. Her heart began to thud. She was going to tell Mr. Joy about Galloping Jim, even though Lucy had begged her not to!

Mr. Joy raised his eyebrows. "Why are you dressed up in your brother's clothes? Are you off on an adventure?"

Sophie blushed. She'd forgotten that girls

would never wear trousers in these days. But the magic carousel obviously thought breeches and a ruffled shirt would be easier for riding through the forest. "Sort of. My name's Sophie. I have some information about Galloping Jim, the robber." She pointed to another copy of the poster which was nailed to the door of the forge.

The blacksmith whistled through his teeth, as though this was exciting news. The constable looked surprised and very serious. "Go on!"

"He's planning to rob Lady Amelia's coach tonight," Sophie explained in a rush. "If you hide in her coach, you could catch him red-handed."

Sophie could see Mr. Joy wasn't sure whether to believe her. She pulled the golden locket from under her cloak. "Look! This proves I'm not making it up."

"It's the Earl of Sussex's stolen locket!" Mr.

Joy turned it over in his hands, then looked up at Sophie. "You say Galloping Jim is planning another robbery tonight?"

"Yes! Lady Amelia is going to a ball, and he's going to wait for her coach at the crossroads."

"Then this is our best chance to catch him!" said Mr. Joy. "No one's ever been able to prove anything against that slippery rogue, but we might just do it! I'm sure Lady Amelia will help us."

Suddenly a small boy in a smart dark green suit ran up. "Message from the manor," he said to the blacksmith. "There was an accident yesterday and the coachman has been hurt. He'll be all right in a few days," he added. "But one of Lady Amelia's carriage ponies put his hoof in a hole and pulled off his shoe. Lady Amelia would like you to go and fit a new one. She won't be going to the ball tonight, not with one of her ponies lame and no coachman to drive her."

The blacksmith told the boy that he'd come to the manor later on. Mr. Joy turned to Sophie. "That's a shame," he said. "We won't be able to catch Galloping Jim if there's no coach for him to rob!"

Sophie felt very disappointed. It had been such a good plan! She thanked Mr. Joy anyway and trailed over to Jewel.

"What's the matter? Didn't he believe you?" asked Jewel, when he saw Sophie looking miserable.

"Lady Amelia can't go to the ball!" Sophie explained. "One of her carriage ponies is lame. We'll have to think of something else."

Jewel didn't say anything for a few moments. Then he scraped the ground with his front hoof. "I could pull the coach, Sophie. If the other pony is about the same size as me, the harness should fit."

Sophie threw her arms around his neck. "Jewel,

that's so brave of you! I know you can do it. Come on, let's go and ask Mr. Joy."

She led Jewel back over to the forge, where the blacksmith was finishing off the last shoe. "Mr. Joy! How big are Lady Amelia's carriage ponies?"

Mr. Joy looked at Jewel. "Well, I'd say they're about the same size as your pony."

"Then Jewel can help pull the coach and we can catch Galloping Jim after all!" Sophie declared. Suddenly she remembered that Mr. Joy was the parish constable, and she shouldn't be ordering him about. She felt her cheeks go bright red, but to her relief Mr. Joy nodded.

"It's a good idea," he said. Then his face fell. "But we've still got no coachman."

Sophie stared at him in dismay. She'd forgotten that Lady Amelia's coach driver had been injured as well! Suddenly she felt Jewel's velvety nose brush against her ear, and his long spiky whiskers tickled her cheek.

"You could drive the coach, Sophie," the pony whispered.

"But I don't know how to!" Sophie whispered back.

Jewel snorted. "I'll look after you. We can do it together. You just need to hold the reins, and I'll tell you what to do. Ask him, go on."

Sophie took a deep breath. "Mr. Joy? If Jewel takes the place of the lame pony, could I drive the coach?" She gazed pleadingly up at the constable.

Mr. Joy looked less sure about this. "Now, I don't know," he said. "There must be someone else we could ask."

Sophie twisted her fingers in Jewel's mane. "But Jewel's my pony—he'd go best with me there to help."

Jewel whinnied, nudging the constable with his nose.

The blacksmith laughed, and Mr. Joy shook

his head, smiling. "Anyone would think that pony understands exactly what we're saying!" he said. "Well, all right, then. As long as I'm there to keep an eye on things, you should be safe. Let's go and see Lady Amelia right now, and tell her she can go to the ball after all."

Sophie grinned and gave Jewel a big hug. They were going to catch Galloping Jim!

Chapter Seven

Constable Joy mounted his sturdy brown and white horse. They led Sophie and Jewel straight to Grey Manor, Lady Amelia's enormous house.

Lady Amelia was in the stable yard, stroking the lame pony. Lady Amelia was very beautiful, a bit younger than Sophie's mom, with curly brown hair piled high on her head. Her red silk dress was so long that it would have trailed on the ground if she hadn't had it looped up over one arm. Sophie could see that she was wearing delicate little red shoes with flowers embroidered on them, but she had wooden sandals strapped on underneath to keep them clean.

Next to Lady Amelia was an older lady who had a very annoyed expression on her face. She was waving a fan and complaining loudly. "Amelia, dear, must we stay here much longer? The smell is simply dreadful. I feel quite ill," she grumbled.

But Lady Amelia was too worried about her lame pony to listen. "Poor Blackberry," she said, reaching over the stable door to rub the pony's nose. "He does look sorry for himself." She turned around and saw Sophie and Mr. Joy leading their ponies across the cobbled yard. "Hello, Mr. Joy. Have you heard about our accident?"

Mr. Joy took off his hat and bowed. "Good day, my lady. Actually, yes. I've come with a plan to help you go to the ball," he said.

"Really?" Lady Amelia looked interested. "Is

this young lady going to help as well? It's so nice to see somebody in sensible clothes—this dress is completely unsuitable for the stable yard." Lady Amelia beamed at Sophie, but the old lady looked horrified.

"Shocking!" she muttered. "A girl in breeches! Whatever next?"

"This is Sophie," said Mr. Joy. "She's the one who's come up with the plan. My lady, we think we can catch Galloping Jim. But we need your help, too."

Lady Amelia clapped her hands. "How exciting!"

Mr. Joy explained how Jewel was going to take the place of the lame pony and Sophie was going to drive the coach so they could catch Galloping Jim red-handed.

"What a brilliant idea!" said Lady Amelia.

The older lady was so shocked that she stopped fanning herself. "Amelia, you can't agree to this dreadful plan! You and this little scrap of a girl, laying a trap for a murderous robber? What nonsense, she's far too young! Oh, I think I'm going to faint. . . ." She swayed, her eyes half closed, but she stood up straight again when it was obvious that no one was going to run over and catch her.

"She loves making a fuss, doesn't she?" Jewel muttered to Sophie. Sophie had to swallow a giggle.

"You simply can't, Amelia. I won't allow it." The older lady shut her fan with a *snap*.

"But, Cousin Flora, we must!" Lady Amelia insisted. "How would you feel if one of your friends was held up by that rogue? And imagine how exciting it will be to tell everyone! You will be a heroine!" She winked at Sophie.

"Oh, do you really think so?" gasped Cousin Flora.

"Of course!" said Mr. Joy.

"We must go and get ready," said Lady Amelia. She led Cousin Flora away before she could change her mind.

Mr. Joy rubbed his hands together. "Well done, Sophie! You stay here, and I'll go and get my eldest boy, Luke. We'll need a strong lad to make sure we can hold Galloping Jim once we catch him."

He got back onto his horse, and Sophie watched them trot out of the stable yard. Jewel nudged her. "Come on, Sophie! You need to find something to wear so you look like a coachman."

Looking around the yard, she spotted a big black coat with gold braid around the sleeves, and a three-cornered hat hanging on a hook behind a door. "Do you think I could borrow those?" she asked.

Jewel nodded. "They must belong to the

injured coachman," he said. "I'm sure he won't mind."

Sophie put them on, rolling up the big sleeves and tipping the hat forward to hide her face. "What do you think?"

"Perfect," Jewel declared. "No one will know you're a girl!"

Sophie waited all afternoon at Grey Manor. The stable boy offered to share his lunch with her, but Sophie was too nervous to eat. Instead, she brushed Jewel until his coat shone like polished coal. The other carriage pony, Shadow, was exactly the same size and color as Jewel, but he didn't have a white diamond on his forehead.

When it started to get dark, Sophie and the stable boy harnessed the ponies to Lady Amelia's carriage. Jewel whispered instructions to Sophie so that she knew how to buckle the leather straps into place. Then they took the carriage around to the front of the house to wait for Lady Amelia and Cousin Flora.

When the two ladies appeared at the top of the steps, Sophie could see why they had needed all afternoon to get ready. Lady Amelia was wearing a magnificent white dress embroidered with flowers made from tiny pearls and silver thread that twinkled as she moved. Her hair was swirled on her head so that it stood up like a tower, and ropes of pearls were woven through it to match the flowers on her dress. Two silver feathers were held in her hair by a diamond clasp. Sophie thought she looked like something out of a fairy tale!

"Good luck, Sophie!" Lady Amelia called before climbing into the coach. Cousin Flora followed her, tucking her rustling lilac skirt around her legs as she sat on the padded velvet seat.

Mr. Joy and Luke ran up the drive just in time, looking rather red faced and breathless. They clambered into the coach and crouched on the floor so that no one could see them. Sophie giggled when she heard Cousin Flora grumbling about sharing a coach with the men. She stroked Jewel's mane, and Shadow's, too, so he didn't feel left out. Feeling very proud, she climbed up to her seat and picked up the reins.

"Let's go!" Sophie slapped the reins lightly on the ponies' backs, and the coach moved forward with a jerk. Sophie gasped with excitement as the wind tugged at her hair.

They were off to catch Galloping Jim!

Chapter Eight

Sophie loved driving Lady Amelia's carriage! Jewel was brilliant at calling instructions to her, telling her when to pull on the reins and when to send the ponies forward at a brisk canter.

Soon they reached the heath. Sophie spotted the tree where she had first seen Galloping Jim's poster, and her heart began to beat faster. She knew the crossroads weren't far ahead.

As they passed the tree with the poster, Jewel whinnied, "Slow down, Sophie! We're almost there!"

Sophie pulled on the reins, and the ponies

slowed to a trot. Suddenly, Galloping Jim shot out in front of them on a tall black horse. He stopped the horse so sharply that it reared up, its front hooves striking the air. "Stand and deliver!" he shouted.

Sophie's heart leaped into her mouth. She could tell Jewel was frightened, too, because his ears were pinned back and his tail swished.

Sophie felt the coach rock beneath her. Mr. Joy and Luke were creeping out of the other door to grab Galloping Jim! She had to distract him so he didn't spot them. Jewel snorted loudly and scraped his hoof on the ground to cover the noise of the coach springs creaking. Sophie was very proud of him.

"Don't hurt us!" she shouted as gruffly as she could.

Galloping Jim threw back his head and roared with laughter. He dismounted and looped his horse's reins over a nearby branch. Then he approached the door of the coach. "Hand over your jewels!" he ordered.

Lady Amelia leaned out of the coach window. She gasped and covered her eyes as Galloping Jim came up. Sophie guessed she was distracting the robber's attention from Mr. Joy and Luke as well. She knew Lady Amelia was much braver than she seemed to be right now.

"Help! Robbers!" Cousin Flora shrieked.

Suddenly there was a scuffling noise, and Mr. Joy and Luke dashed around the coach behind Galloping Jim. He let out a shout, but Mr. Joy threw a sack over his head before he could run away. The robber kicked and struggled as Luke tied a rope around his arms. He was caught!

Sophie hopped down from the coachman's box and opened the coach door with a bow. "Lady Amelia, we have a guest for you!"

Mr. Joy and Luke heaved Galloping Jim onto the floor of the coach. He lay in a heap, wriggling and muttering.

Lady Amelia beamed. "Excellent! I've always thought this coach could do with a footstool. Don't you agree, Cousin Flora?"

"Oh yes," said Cousin Flora, looking much braver now that Galloping Jim was tied up. And both ladies placed their dainty dancing shoes on the robber's back!

"That's a job well done," said Mr. Joy, climbing into the coach. "Luke, you ride Galloping Jim's horse back to the forge. Sophie, let's get this villain under lock and key!"

Sophie pushed back her three-cornered hat and threw her arms around Jewel's neck. "You were so brave! And you were wonderful, too, Shadow!"

She jumped back onto the coachman's box

and clicked her tongue to send the ponies forward. They'd caught Galloping Jim! Lucy wouldn't have to live with her horrid uncle anymore!

Lucy was waiting in the village square when they returned, wrapped in a warm cloak and holding a lantern. She looked amazed when she saw Sophie driving Lady Amelia's coach. When Mr. Joy dragged out his struggling prisoner, she gasped. "Uncle Jim!"

"He tried to hold up the coach," Sophie explained. "I know you didn't want me to tell Mr. Joy, but I had to!"

Lucy nodded sadly. "I know you did."

"Where will you go?" Sophie asked.

Lucy shrugged. "I don't know. I don't have any other relatives. Perhaps I'll have to go to the poorhouse."

Sophie wasn't sure what the poorhouse was,

but it sounded horrible. Her heart sank. Had she and Jewel just made things worse for Lucy? Jewel blew softly in her ear and Sophie patted him, feeling tears prick in her eyes.

"Nonsense!" Mr. Joy came back from locking Lucy's uncle in a shed at the back of his cottage. "You can move in with us, Lucy. Mrs. Joy and I have always wanted a daughter."

Lucy's face lit up. "Really? Thank you so much!"

Sophie felt very pleased for her. Now Lucy would never be lonely again. And even better, she wouldn't have to rob any more coaches or look after her horrid uncle.

Lady Amelia leaned out of her carriage. "Congratulations, Sophie! You and your brave pony should be very proud of yourselves." She opened her little beaded purse. "Here, take this." She handed Sophie a shining golden coin. "Well done, my dear."

Sophie blushed and stroked Jewel, who

snorted and tossed his head. "I can feel the magic tugging us back to the carousel," he said. "Quick, you need to unharness me." Sophie undid the straps and led him out from between the shafts of the carriage. His saddle was still at Grey Manor, so she climbed on bareback, leaning down to give Lucy one last hug good-bye.

"Will you come back one day?" Lucy called as she trotted away.

"I hope so!" Sophie called back. "Good-bye! Good-bye, everyone!"

She hung on tight as Jewel cantered out of the village. He didn't slow down even when the dark, shadowy woods loomed around them. Sophie smiled as she remembered how nervous he'd been at the start of their journey. As she reached down to give him a pat, the misty shadows seemed to draw closer and change color.

Now Sophie and Jewel were galloping through

a silvery-pink cloud of sparkles. Sophie felt Jewel's gallop steady into a gentle rise and fall. The mist cleared, and Sophie found she was gripping a twisty golden pole. Jewel's shining coat was black paint again, and she was sitting on a wooden saddle. She could see her parents and Molly waving to her as the Magic Pony Carousel slowed down. The adventure was over.

Sophie dismounted, and went to stroke Jewel's nose one last time. As she opened her fingers, she saw a glint of gold. It was Lady Amelia's golden coin!

Sophie clutched it tight and put her face close to Jewel's wooden ear. "I'll never forget you, ever!" she whispered happily.

Gallop away with **Magic Pony Carousel**
Book 5: Flame the Desert Pony

Chapter One

The fairground looked lovely in the misty morning light. It was in Chloe's local park, at the bottom of a hill. She gazed down on the colorful rides in delight as she and her dad made their way to the entrance.

"Come on—let's find an exciting ride!" she cried as soon as they were inside the gates.

"Don't you want to get a hot dog first?" her dad asked.

Chloe loved hot dogs. She was about to say

yes, but one of the rides suddenly caught her eye. She gasped.

"*Barker's Magic Pony Carousel,*" she read out loud.

The carousel was painted in red, gold, and silver swirls, and the beautiful wooden ponies moved gracefully up and down under rows of twinkling lights. Chloe couldn't tear her eyes away!

"Is that a no?" teased her dad.

"Do you think I could have a hot dog *after* trying the carousel?" Chloe said.

"Oh, I think so," her dad said. "Why don't you go and get on board? We can find a hot dog stand after you've had your ride."

"Thanks, Dad," Chloe said happily. She didn't have any brothers or sisters to play with, but her dad made sure that she never felt lonely. He was always taking her to do fun things, and at home they liked reading mysterious detective stories together.

She skipped over to the carousel to choose a pony. The ride had just slowed to a halt, and one pony seemed to be gazing right at her. It was a stunning golden palomino with a creamy mane and tail and beautiful big brown eyes. From its pretty face with its slightly upturned nose, Chloe knew it must be an Arabian pony, and by the look of the saddle and bridle it could have come straight out of the desert!

She ran forward for a closer look. The pony's saddle was covered in deep ruby-red velvet with a golden fringe all the way around the edge. The matching ruby saddlecloth was embroidered with palm trees and birds in shiny gold thread. Red and gold tassels dangled from the edge, and there were matching tassels on the breastplate and bridle.

"Wow!" Chloe exclaimed. At her local riding

school, she loved helping to get ponies ready for shows. She wasn't a very confident rider yet, but she was really good at braiding manes and weaving pretty ribbons into the hair. She looked closely at the gorgeous saddlecloth. Whoever had made this must love decorating ponies as much as she did!

"Hello there!" said a deep, friendly voice.

Chloe whirled around and saw a tall man stepping down from the carousel. He was wearing a red velvet suit lined with green silk and a stripy red and green top hat.

"Hello," said Chloe. "Are you Mr. Barker?"

"I am indeed!" said Mr. Barker, his eyes sparkling. "Would you like to ride on my splendid carousel?"

Chloe nodded. "Yes, please. I'd like to ride the palomino, if that's okay."

Mr. Barker stroked his chin. "Well, that's fine

by me," he said, "but we'll have to see what the carousel thinks."

"The carousel?" Chloe was puzzled.

Mr. Barker tapped his nose and leaned toward her. "It's a *magic* carousel, remember!" he whispered. Then he reached out and took a bright orange balloon from a passing balloon seller. With a flourish, he pulled a little pony-shaped badge out of his lapel. "Now, Chloe, let's see if your wish can come true!"

Before Chloe had time to wonder how Mr. Barker could possibly know her name, he burst the balloon with the badge pin. *POP!* Chloe stared in amazement as a little pink ticket fluttered to the ground.

Mr. Barker beamed at her. "I think you'll find there's something written on it," he said.

Chloe could just see some swirly silver writing on one side of the ticket. She bent down to pick it up. "'*Flame*,'" she read, then looked up at Mr. Barker.

"What a coincidence!" he said with a wink.

Chloe ran over to the palomino. There was a name written on the pretty red headband. She stood on tiptoe to read it.

"'Flame'!" she exclaimed.

Chapter Two

"All aboard!" cried Mr. Barker. "Step up, step up for the most exciting ride of your lives! The Magic Pony Carousel is about to start!"

Quickly Chloe scrambled up onto Flame's back. She had read books about different kinds of ponies, and she knew Arabians came from the desert, where they had to be strong and fast to race long distances over the sand.

She patted Flame's shiny wooden neck, then held on tight to the twisty golden pole. The carousel began to turn, moving her gently up and down. Chloe thought about what it would be like to ride across the desert with the sun beating down. She could almost feel the warm rays on her skin . . . but then the air began to shimmer, and Chloe saw swirls of pink glitter falling around her. She rubbed her eyes. She must be imagining things! But no—the glitter was still falling softly.

"Ow!" she exclaimed, as specks flew into her face. "What's that?"

She looked down and saw grains of sand dusting the pommel of the saddle. "Sand?" she muttered, brushing it away with her hand. "I can't be imagining *that*!"

The glitter began to clear, and she tried to grab the twisty golden pole again—but it had disappeared! Instead, her hands landed on a soft, silky mane. Chloe nearly fell out of the saddle in surprise. Hastily she steadied herself on the saddle's high pommel and picked up the red leather reins. What was going on? She wasn't sitting on a carousel at all now. Flame was a real, live pony!

The fairground had vanished. Instead, there was golden, shimmering sand as far as she could see. She and Flame were galloping between the rolling dunes of a desert.

"Steady!" cried Chloe. She had never ridden this fast before! She gave a little tug on the reins and Flame slowed down to a canter. But the sand was still flying into her face, so Chloe pulled on the reins again, slowing the pony to a trot. She groped for the pocket of her fleecy pink cardigan, looking for a handkerchief to hold over her nose. To her astonishment, the pocket wasn't there. She glanced down. She wasn't wearing her cardigan at all!

Chloe was wearing a pale blue cotton gown

embroidered with pretty yellow cross stitches. There was a little kerchief around her neck in rich sky blue, decorated with a fringe of tiny red and blue beads. Chloe quickly lifted it up to cover her nose and mouth. It would keep the sand out perfectly. Then she reached up and patted her hair. Phew! She was still wearing her favorite barrette decorated with rainbow-colored butterflies. This was all very mysterious but exciting, too!

As Flame's hooves thudded across the golden sand, Chloe saw that they were approaching a little town. All the houses were whitewashed, and many of them had domed roofs that stood out against the blue sky. In the brilliant sunshine, they were almost too bright to look at. Chloe shaded her eyes with one hand as Flame reached the edge of the town.

They trotted down a narrow street, and

Chloe spotted a man leading a donkey laden with baskets of vegetables. She reined Flame to a walk and followed the donkey over the smooth cobbles. The street opened into a square with palm trees in the middle, surrounding a stone well. All around the edge of the square were colorful, busy market stalls.

"Wow!" said Chloe. "What a great place!"

"Yes, isn't it?" agreed a soft voice.

Chloe looked around, wondering who had spoken. There wasn't anyone nearby. With a shrug, she nudged Flame forward, looking at the different market stalls. There were richly woven rugs and hangings, mounds of scented spices, wonderful fabrics, and clothes.

"Figs! Lovely plump figs!" called one stall owner. He smiled at Chloe and held one out to her.

She laughed and shook her head. The fig

looked delicious, but she didn't have any money.

A woman wearing a bright red shawl walked past with a pail of water balanced on her head. The sight of the crystal-clear water made Chloe realize how thirsty she was.

"Oh! I'd love a drink," she exclaimed out loud.

"So would I!"

It was the mysterious voice again! Chloe peered around, but no one seemed to be taking any notice of her. Shaking her head, she slipped down from Flame's back and led the pony over to the palm trees beside the well. She tied Flame's reins to a wooden post.

"I won't be a minute, Flame," she said, patting the pony's neck. Then she headed toward the well. A group of girls was waiting with stone jars for their turn to draw water.

"Hey!" called the voice again.

Chloe spun around. There was no one behind her, just Flame tied to the post.

"Please could I have a drink, too?" begged the voice. "It was very hot galloping across the desert!"

Chloe stared hard. Could it be . . . ? She stepped forward. "Flame," she whispered. "Was that you?"

The palomino blinked her big brown eyes. "Of course it was!" she said.

Chloe flung her arms around her neck. "You can talk!" she cried. "This is the best carousel ride ever!"

Flame nuzzled Chloe's cheek. "I can talk, but the ticket you picked with my name on it means that only you will be able to understand me," she said. "The carousel has sent us here to help someone and solve a problem. I'm not sure what it is, though. We'll have to find that out for ourselves."

Chloe had a worrying thought. "What about my dad? He won't know where I've gone!"

Flame shook her long silky mane. "Don't worry," she said. "When we get back, it will be as if we've never been away."

"Wow!" breathed Chloe. "My very own magical adventure with my very own Arabian pony!"

"That's right," agreed Flame. "A very *thirsty* Arabian pony!"

Climb aboard the
Magic Pony Carousel!

Sparkle
1

THE KNIGHT'S PONY

Star
3
THE WESTERN PONY

Flame
5
THE DESERT PONY

HarperTrophy®
An Imprint of HarperCollinsPublishers

www.harpercollinschildrens.com